Mr. Brown Can MOO!

Can You?

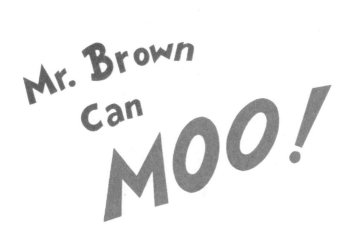

Mr. Brown
Can
MOO!

Can You?

By
Dr. Seuss

A Bright & Early Book
RANDOM HOUSE / NEW YORK

Oh, the wonderful things
Mr. Brown can do!
He can go like a cow.
He can go **Moo Moo**
Mr. Brown can do it.
How about you?

He can go like a bee.

Mr. Brown can

How about you?
Can you go

He can go like horse feet

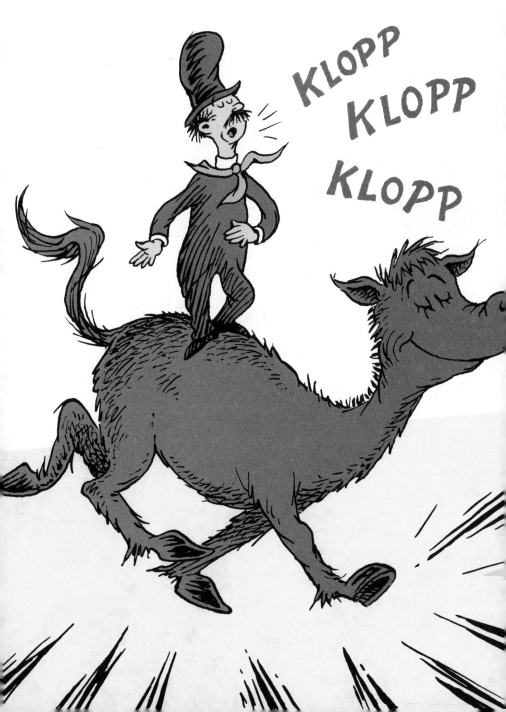

KLOPP
KLOPP
KLOPP

He can go

EEK
EEK

like a squeaky shoe.

He can go
like a rooster . . .

COCK A
DOODLE
DOO

He can go
like an owl . . .

HOO HOO
HOO HOO

EEK EEK
EEK EEK
COCK-A-DOODLE-DOO
HOO HOO HOO HOO

How about you?

He can go
like the rain . . .

DIBBLE DIBBLE
DIBBLE DOPP

He can go like a train

CHOO CHOO
CHOO
CHOO
CHOO

Oh, the wonderful things
Mr. Brown can do!

Moo Moo
Buzz Buzz
Pop Pop Pop
Eek Eek
Hoo Hoo
Klopp Klopp Klopp
Dibble Dibble
Dopp Dopp
Cock-a-Doodle-Doo

Mr. Brown can do it.
How about you?

. . . like the soft,
soft whisper
of a butterfly.

Maybe YOU can, too.
I think you ought to try.

He can go
like a horn. . .

BLURP
BLURP
BLURP
BLURP

. . . like a big cat drinking

He can go like a clock.
He can

He can

He can go
like a hand
on a door . . .

Oh, the wonderful things
Mr. Brown can do!

BLURP BLURP
SLURP SLURP

COCK-A-DOODLE-DOO

KNOCK KNOCK KNOCK

and HOO HOO HOO

He can even

SIZZLE
SIZZLE

He can do that, too,
like an egg
in a frying pan.
How about you?

Mr. Brown is smart,
as smart as they come!
He can do
a hippopotamus
chewing gum!

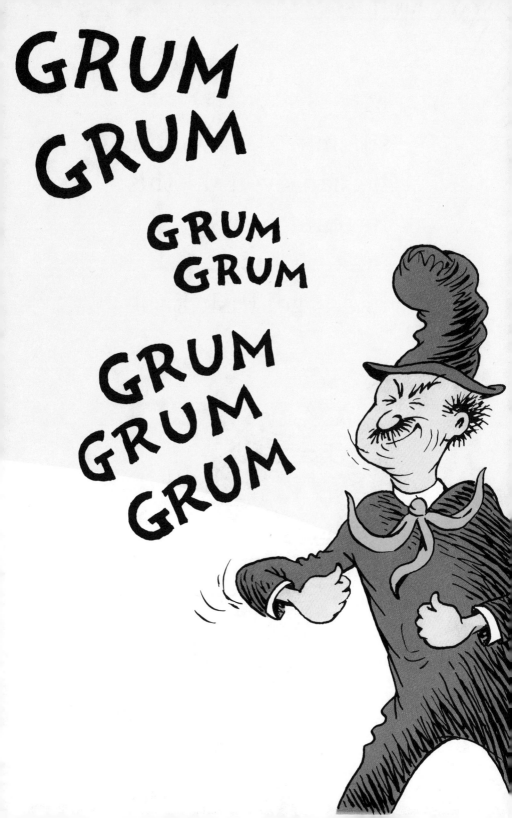

Mr. Brown is
so smart
he can even do this:
he can even
make a noise
like a goldfish kiss!

BOOM BOOM BOOM

Mr. Brown is a wonder!

BOOM BOOM BOOM

Mr. Brown makes thunder!

He makes lightning!

SPLATT SPLATT SPLATT

And it's very, very hard
to make a noise like that.

Oh, the wonderful things
Mr. Brown can do!

Moo Moo
Buzz Buzz
Pop Pop Pop

    Eek Eek
    Hoo Hoo
    Klopp Klopp Klopp

Dibble Dibble
Dopp Dopp
Cock-a-Doodle-Doo

    Grum Grum
    Grum Grum
    Choo Choo Choo

Boom Boom
Splatt Splatt
Tick Tick Tock

    Sizzle Sizzle
    Blurp Blurp
    Knock Knock Knock

A SLURP and a WHISPER
and a FISH KISS, too.

Mr. Brown can do it.
How about YOU?